Review

Charlie & Lola: A Tale Of Two Squirrels is an enjoyable and exciting story filled with interesting characters. The sequel to *The Life of Charlie Ryan: A Squirrels Tale*, this story continues to follow Charlie and introduces new characters who embark on a new adventure. A funny and heartwarming story with friendship at the centre, the story will be enjoyed by children and adults alike. My favourite part was when Charlie and Lola met, because it was fascinating when someone else tells the story.

I loved this book because of its interesting facts and amazing storyline. I loved the characters, especially how they act and their personalities. They are funny because of what they talk about. I especially like the cat Smudge.

It really inspires me to write interesting stories and I'm sure it will also inspire everyone else that reads this wonderful tale. I would love for there to be another sequel to this marvellous book as I really want to know what happens next. I am extremely curious to find out more about the twin squirrels and what the future holds for the Ryan family.

*. *. *. *. *

Lucy McIntosh - 9-years-old

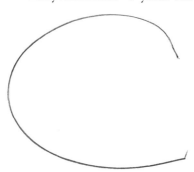

Charlie & Lola:
A Tale of Two Squirrels

Sheralee Ryan

This paperback edition published 2022 by Jasami Publishing Ltd
an imprint of Jasami Publishing Ltd
Glasgow, Scotland
https://jasamipublishingltd.com

ISBN 978-1-913798-50-5

Visit JasamiPublishingLtd.com to read more about all our books and to purchase them. You will also find features, author information and news of any events, also be the first to hear about our new releases.

Jasami Acknowledgements

Illustrator
Holly Richards

Editor
Amy Young

Acknowledgements

*For Charlie who continues to inspire me, and to
Lola for bursting into our lives.
Also, Gary and Keryn who believed in me.
Thank you to the Jasami team who have made it
all happen, I am eternally grateful.*

Dedication

As always, for our daughter Keryn Ryan who has an abundance of love for all God's creatures.

Contents

Prologue

This sequel to *The Life of Charlie Ryan: A Squirrel's Tale* is the real life continuing adventures of Charlie Ryan, introducing Lola Ryan, and the observations of Smudge Ryan. These adventures are elaborated and embroidered upon by Charlie's adopted Mom in order to expand the personalities, habits and observance of the Sun Squirrels that live in the Kalumbila forest in North West Province of Zambia. This story, as the first, is intended to show readers that the animal kingdom has many emotions similar to that of us fellow earth dwellers. The most powerful of all is *LOVE*. Charlie is a gentle, caring and loving soul, and although Lola begins as an independent, strong and imprudent character she learns about love from those around her. Smudge, the oldest Ryan in the household of furry creatures has earned her status as the senior member of the Ryan pets however she does think her title holds more significance than it really does.

Charlie & Lola's Family

Dad	Gary
Mom	Sheralee
Sister	Keryn
Dog brothers	Homer & Sheki (twin brothers)
Dog sisters	Gazi and Nama
Cat sisters	Licorice and Smudge
Blind bird	Lilo
Owl	Bila
Owl	Kalum

Both Bila and Kalum were rehabilitated and released. All the injured wild animals who come to the Ryan home are released once they are completely rehabilitated.

Do You Know?

A Sun Squirrel can only be found in sub-Saharan Africa. They get their name from the fact that they are always seeking out a warm spot where they bask in the sun.

A drey is the name given to a squirrels nest which is usually made in the hollow of a tree.

Smarties are different coloured, sugar-coated chocolate confectionery that look like buttons.

A baby squirrel is called a kitten.

A chameleon is a slow moving lizard-like creature that has an extendable tongue like an elastic band, and they can move their eyes independently as well as have the ability to change colour in order to blend in with their surroundings.

A lesser bush baby is a small type of primate that is found in the forests of sub-Saharan Africa. They are nocturnal animals meaning they are active at night, have very large round eyes and can move their ears independently.

A legavaan is a very large rock monitor lizard from Africa that can grow up to two meters in length.

An owl has three eyelids: one for blinking, one for sleeping, and one for keeping the eye clean and healthy.

Masuku are wild fruits that grow in Zambia. They are sweet-tasting, have a hard outside and a seed in the middle.

The Zambian bush is the uncultivated, wild foliage that covers the ground, and the tall trees are higher than six men standing on each others shoulders reaching up to the sky. The untamed forest is home to the dangerous and venomous snakes as well other creatures that are unique to this area. There are anthills larger than a small house and during the rainy season all that is brown and dry turns to a lush green after the first downpour.

Sheralee Ryan

I Am Lola Ryan

I Am Lola Ryan

I suppose that makes me an adopted member of the Ryan family - just like Charlie. Although we have never met and do not share the same birth parents, we are both Sun Squirrels and like Charlie, I came to live with the Ryan family after being rescued by humans.

My real mother always said I was going to be trouble. You see I'm fierce, I'm fearless and I am a mighty girl. So, one day when the starlings were out being cheeky to everyone and harassing whoever they came across for fun in the forest, I climbed to the top of the tree and gave them a piece of my mind. The leader of the flock almost fell to the ground in shock mid-flight. I told him he was mean, ugly and the forest didn't need any of them. The starlings take up space and waste the good, clean air! My mom, shivering down below on a branch, yelled at me to get under cover and in that moment of distraction, the starling swooped me up and carried me off in his sharp beak. I remember being mad at the indignity of it and ordered him to put me down. So, he did. Just like that, I was dropped from the sky and landed in someone's garden close to a tree. I miraculously avoided hitting obstacles on the way down and survived the fall, landing on the soft grass.

A human hand reached out and I was taken to a safe place where I didn't even have to move to get food or drink. I was given a soft, warm blanket to rest my aching body and it wasn't long before I received a warm bottle of milk. I suppose I did still need my mom and she was right about me being trouble. I knew I'd gone too far this time and I cried for days wanting to be back with my squirrel family. I was afraid to go outside and stayed behind the safety of the walls of the human house that I found myself in. The house became my new world, and it didn't take long for me to explore every inch of it. The curtains were my trees and reaching the top, while still having a roof to protect me from those mean starlings, was the best. I could run up and down, jump from curtain to sofa and back again without a care in the world.

But squirrels are naturally curious and adventurous. It didn't take long before I was bored. I longed for the outside. I longed for the tall trees of the Kalumbila forest and the fresh breeze I remembered so well as I raced through the trees with my mom. Squirrels just aren't meant to be inside all the time. I had to make a plan and get my mind right so I could be my fierce, fearless, mighty self.

I Don't Like Humans

One night, after the sun had gone to sleep and I was curled up warm and cozy in my blanket, I was taken to another place. Being sleepy, and because, of course, squirrels don't like the dark, I just went back to dreamland hoping one day my dreams would become my reality. Early morning, and I mean as the sun cracks the night and chases it away, I poked my head out of the blanket and all was the same yet very different.

The smells were different, as were the sounds, but it all looked the same. I began to think I was having a nightmare. I could hear dogs making a raucous and there on the couch lay a cat! Later, I found out her name was Licorice. She opened one lazy cat's eye and then both eyes sprang open as if she had been poked! I just looked at her and she got up and moved away muttering "not another one!" as she scurried out of the lounge. I had no idea what her problem was, but it was my first taste of the power I have as a mighty squirrel. I didn't have to do a thing or say a word, I just gave my "squirrel look" and the cat moved. What power I have. I can rule the world!

It didn't take me long to explore this new house and find out more about who lived in it. Four dogs came hurtling through the door and skidded to a halt in front of me. The two brothers looked identical. They must be twins, but because I am a smart squirrel I could see the difference, one called Homer and one called Sheki. I saw Homer push Sheki and

Sheki push back and so the fight began. Gazi, the oldest, told them to stop but they didn't. I found out very quickly that Sheki and Homer never listen. Nama, the fourth dog, took one long look at me and skated down the passage on the polished floors with her tail between her legs. My mom, I call her that now because she is the closest I have found anyone to be to my real squirrel mom, came from where Nama had disappeared and laughed. I decided there and then that I would only love my mom (later I included my dad too). Everyone else was against me and I refused to like any more than those two humans, my mom and dad.

I especially did not like Gertrude. She is the person who comes to help clean the house. One day she was pulling this silly, sucking contraption around behind her and she deliberately sucked up all the peanuts and jelly tots that I had so carefully collected and piled up. It had taken me ages to collect so many. I had a plan for them, and she just came along and sucked them up. Disbelief turned to rage and I ran at her and bit her on the leg. Gertrude screamed and ran - the next thing my mom was there. She picked me up so I bit her too and the blood flowed red and fast. She held me tight and kissed my head saying soothing things in my ear. I calmed down and stopped squirming to get out of her grip. That's why I decided my mom was just the best. No matter what I did, no matter how angry I got, even though she was upset with my behaviour she just showed me love and showered me with kisses telling me it was alright. We all need someone to love us unconditionally even though they might not understand or even agree with what we say or do. It would take me a long time to be less angry towards humans, but that love eventually got me there. That and perhaps me growing up a bit!

However, I never came to forgive Gertrude and every opportunity I got, especially once I was back in the forest, I would return home to find her and if she was outside I would chase her back inside. Once, it was all so very quiet and the peanut table was nearly empty, and this was now the second day no one had come to replenish it. I was starting to get annoyed, even with my mom. What was she doing that was more important than making sure my peanut supply was uninterrupted? I hopped through the window and the house was empty. Those lazy cats were lounging about on the sofa as usual, but they don't count. Lilo was resting on her perch in the kitchen. Lilo is an old bird and although I do like her, I don't much bother with her. We seem to speak a different language. She knows so much but she talks so slowly and sometimes tells the same stories over and over again. I have a lot of respect for old Lilo but when peanut provisions are dire, I must take immediate action. Her story would have to wait for another time.

As I lay in the fold of the kitchen window blinds, Gertrude appeared. I demanded to know what happened to my humans, but she stood like a statue with her eyes and mouth wide open. I fluffed my tail, which is totally necessary to express my anger, and hurled myself at her hoping I wouldn't miss. I did. Gertrude can move when she wants to. She ran out the front door and around the house. I gave chase. Squirrels can move much faster than humans ever possibly could, but Gertrude outsmarted me. She ran back inside through the back door and closed all the doors and windows so I couldn't get in, so I marched up and down the verandah looking for an open window. What I should have done was rush around to the bedroom side and hop through one of those open windows, but I only thought of that while raging up and down out front and heard the windows slam shut one after the other until Gertrude was her own prisoner, and I was left outside to guard her. I continued to rage up and down on guard duty until it started to get dark, and then totally unlike me, I gave up. Gertrude had won this battle but next time I would be better prepared. Gertrude one - Lola zero. I would have to even the score.

I Like Sparkly Things

My mom used to wear the most exquisite cross made with precious, yellow gems with a diamond in the centre that glistened and shone from where it hung around her neck. I knew I just had to have that piece of jewellery for myself. I would lie awake dreaming of the glittering, sparkly yellow and the flashing white of the diamond. I needed those gems so badly I could almost feel the cool, jagged edges of each stone that had been moulded into the yellow metal of the cross. It was the same gold as the chain that tied it to my mom's neck. Whenever I got the chance, I would sit on my mom's shoulder and admire the glorious sight nestled on her chest close to where I could hear her heartbeat. I plotted and planned and schemed and connived until finally, I cannot even remember how it happened or what came over me, but I chomped down so hard on the yellow chain that it tumbled down like a weightless line in slow motion towards the ground.

In a flash, I realised I would lose my precious trinket to the earth's magnetic pull if I didn't act immediately. I nosedived from my mom's shoulder while she watched helplessly as I lunged for the cross. I snatched it up in my teeth and scampered up the curtain to the top railing. After much chasing and shouting Mom got her precious charm back and I watched her put it away in the wooden box on top of the chest of drawers in her bedroom. That made me a little happier knowing neither of us would have it - I would make it all mine. I hopped out the window, not wanting to show my disappointment in losing it or to give away any sign of the devious new plan I was hatching in my head. I would revisit the wooden box one day when all were preoccupied or otherwise engaged.

Squirrels can be easily distracted and it is thought that they are cute, cuddly and very sweet little creatures. I am not one of those stereotypical squirrels. I hold on to a thought or a feeling and own it, keeping it in my heart forever. I can look cute when I want to, but in a split second I will bare my teeth and growl louder than an angry mongrel when cornered or pushed too far. That's me - fierce, fearless, mighty Lola. It takes some intelligence to understand that being fearless does not mean being reckless. I have to keep my wits about me at all times, especially in the forest where I have made my own little nest called a drey.

The day began with a beautiful, hot and humid morning. The sun glistened through the rain drops that were clinging to the leaves as if afraid their final destination to the ground would be their last.

I sat in the tree next to the peanut table in our garden and thought how my real Mom, my squirrel Mom, would have loved to watch the sun's sparkles in the water droplets. I imagined so hard that I could see her perfectly right in front of my eyes and had to blink hard to bring myself back to reality. I held my eyes tightly closed and opened them slowly. There she was still in front of me not moving at all. I wondered if I was perhaps going mad.

My imagination had taken over and my dreams were as if I was watching a television programme about squirrels. Without realising, I called out her name and she ran towards me nearly knocking me right off my branch. It was all real. My dear squirrel mother had found me and we danced around, mother and daughter together again at last. I had so much to ask her. So much to tell. She could not believe it was me and she kept sniffing me and cuddling me. Normally I would have said that it's so not cool to mollycoddle me at my age and also not to forget I am the fearless, fierce, mighty Lola. This time I didn't say a word. I just felt an immense amount of gratitude in my heart that this was my squirrel mom and nothing would ever part us again. There were cheers from all around and lots of little squirrel heads began appearing from behind tree trunks and large leaves joining in the happy, momentous reunion of our friendship, loyalty, and abundant love. I couldn't wait to show my mom my new home which was big enough for both of us to live in. Just as well, as my mom told me the beautiful big tree on the other side of the forest where she had her drey, fell over in the recent storm and she had not had time to find a new, safe tree to make a new home. It was as if it was meant to be. We raced through the trees to the wild bush next to the big house where I had built my nest.

Meanwhile elsewhere in the forest…

Charlie Ryan's Calling

I am Charlie Ryan, a squirrel with the human touch. I was rescued and raised by my human family and I am as happy and free as all squirrels should be. I stayed with my human family, with dogs and cats, plus a blind bird, Lilo, for as long as I could. Then one day, deep down in my little squirrel heart there was a calling so strong that I just could not ignore it. A calling to the wild forests of Kalumbila. I also had a personal quest of my own, and that was to go in search of the Smartie tree. I decided it would be best if I didn't share my plans with anyone just in case they tried to talk me out of it. Also, I did not want to be sad when I was going on an adventure of such an epic proportion. I needed to keep my wits about me. So, one morning after a really good sleep, I ate as much as I could, hopped out the window and headed for the trees. I heard my mom calling my name. Nothing ever gets past her. I sat in the tree looking down on her and promised

I'd be back soon. She seemed happy, smiling up at me, so off I went from branch to branch and tree to tree, singing my own little tune as I scampered along until I ran out of breath. By then I was quite far from home, and I wondered if I'd made the right decision.

I reasoned with myself, telling myself that I am all grown up now. I'm no longer a kitten - baby squirrels are called kittens and they stay with their real moms for two or three months before they go off on their own. I have been with my human family for nine months now and that makes me an adult. I have much to learn out here in the forest and wild bush of Zambia, especially about climbing trees; there was no one in the Ryan family who knew how to do that well. Especially not Homer and Sheki, my fox terrier brothers. I knew I would miss them the most and it was a pity they couldn't come on this escapade with me. Somehow in my heart I just knew I had to go on this adventure alone.

While I sat on the branch of a very leafy tree, I started to get that feeling of being watched. I looked about and at the same time tried to remain frozen in place. That's not easy to do I can tell you! Just as I relaxed the leaves moved and my eyes were seeing something my brain couldn't explain. The question was should I stay or should I run as fast as squirrel legs can run, and they can run quite fast when they need to! I tensed myself, ready to spring off the branch and flee, when I heard a chuckle and saw that the green form, of what looked like the leaves, changed colour to a whiteish yellow and begin to shake with laughter.

It was an old chameleon and he thought it hilarious that I didn't know what he was. I felt quite foolish and explained to him that it was my first ever encounter with such a creature, and what a cool creature the chameleon is. Not only can he change colour when he wants to, but his eyes can move in all directions all at once.

That means Mr. Chameleon can look in front and behind all at the same time. What is also quite amazing is his feet look just like the thing my mom uses when she dishes up salad for the family at dinner time. I asked him how come he changes colour and he told me that there are lots of dangerous creatures in the forest who love the taste of chameleon. The only way to stay safe is to blend in and keep very, very still. I asked him why not just run as fast as his salad tong feet could run, and he explained that chameleons are not very athletic at all. They do not move fast for anything or anybody. I humphed and thought that was really quite silly, but we are all different and have our own really cool things that we can do. I would love to blend into my surroundings. It's like a disappearing act. One minute you are there and then poof you are not!

A New Home

After saying goodbye to the old chameleon, I dawdled along the branches pretending I was invisible. Every time I heard a noise I froze, no matter what position I was in. I thought I was getting quite good at it until there was a noise so loud it frightened me right off my branch and I landed on the soft leaves and grass below. Thinking I might have broken myself somewhere, I lay there looking up at the sky and noticed it was dark grey and threatening to burst with rain. That big noise was thunder. Thunder doesn't usually frighten me but it came so unexpectedly and it seemed so much louder and closer now that I was far, far away from home. That's what got me thinking about where I would sleep for the night. Squirrels don't like the dark, or the cold or the wet. Soon I would be all of those things if I didn't act quickly and smartly. Still being in the ground, I sprang to my feet again and scurried up the nearest big tree.

Quite high up in the trunk of the tree was a hollow that was big enough for me, and luckily for me, it was empty. It felt just right especially when I curled myself up into a tight, little ball and put my tail around my head. All I needed was a soft, warm blanket like I had in my bed at home.

My heart felt saddened that I wasn't at home. I knew my family would be feeling anxious by now too. Mom would have to explain that all wild animals need to be exactly where God intended them to be, and I just knew that they would all understand. Besides, I did plan to visit and let them know I was alive and well. Right at the present moment I needed a few comforts in my new home and I had just the right idea in mind for that. Somehow my brain just told me which leaves were perfect for my bed in my new home. I raced to the tree that matched the picture in my mind, and sure enough the leaves were there. Lovely, soft, velvety leaves pretty much like my blanket only better. I used my teeth and clipped off a twig with lots of fresh leaves on it and hurried back to the hole in the big tree, where I lined the bottom neatly and then scooted back to get more. I layered the leaves one on top of the other until I had the perfect squirrel nest. My mom would be so proud if she could see it. Just as I put the last leaf in and curled myself into the space, the thunder exploded loudly and lightning flashed bright white across the sky. Rain pelted down as if the sky had suddenly been changed to water and couldn't hold itself up anymore. It rained hard and for a long time. I stayed curled up warm and dry, my own little squirrel heart bursting with pride at what I had accomplished all on my own. I remember my mom telling Keryn once that there were so many things she could do on her own that would make her feel strong, confident and secure. That's exactly how I felt at this moment in my life. With that in mind I fell fast asleep listening to the thunder and the rain and my happy heart thumping. Sweet dreams, I said to myself.

Danger All Around

There are lots of dangerous creatures all around in the Kalumbila forest and many of them come out of their hiding places after dark. I think that's why squirrels don't like the dark and prefer to be in the safety of their homes as soon as the sun goes to sleep. I know my mom always used to tell me I had to sleep in the big house with the door and window shut in my room to keep me safe. There was a night when a big, strange, orange cat came into our house. Nama was the first to notice and she performed like a circus clown, which of course excited the others and they all began to make noise. Lights went on and everyone was told to calm down. The orange cat took off through the window and up the driveway then disappeared into the dark night. My mom said he was coming for Licorice and Smudge's food. The next day she put a bowl of cat biscuits by the gate so he didn't have to come and disturb us in the middle of the night when he wanted a snack.

I wondered why he didn't just stay at his own home and eat his own biscuits. Maybe Smudge and Licorice have nicer biscuits. I tried them to see for myself and they are quite good, if there is nothing else to eat. Squirrels love trying new things but it's not always a good experience. I found out that humans like to take things called tablets sometimes when they are not feeling too well. I broke into a silver and plastic card of tablets once and they all had terrible tasting powder inside each pill. My mom was really worried about me that day. I never saw another tablet ever again after that. I had already decided I wouldn't ever eat another one, but it seemed my mom was not going to let me anyway and all the tablets got hidden away from me.

Some nights the moon is so big and bright it looks like if I go to the top of the tallest tree, I might actually be able to stretch up and touch it.

It looks like a ginormous tablet in the night sky, and if it tastes anything like the tablets I tasted at home I shall leave it well alone. This one particular night the moon was shining brightly and I could hear many worrying noises coming from all corners of the forest as the nocturnal animals come out to play. It was on this night that I hunkered down as much as I could in my little hollow in the tree. I missed my family so very much as I trembled, fearing the morning would never arrive. I did fall asleep, and usually squirrels sleep like the dead, but on this night my nerves were on edge so when an incredibly fluffy weight landed on me, I was wide awake and pushing and shoving as if my life depended on it. Turned out it was a lesser bush baby, which really is one of the cutest little creatures I ever saw.

She was running for her life with a very large, spotted eagle-owl hot on her tail. She begged me to keep quiet and let her stay put in the hollow of the tree whilst danger lurked nearby. I could hear the owl in the branches up above calling to his mates and it was very scary indeed. The little bush baby curled her beautiful, long soft tail around me and I fell fast asleep feeling warm, loved and protected by my new friend. Just before the sun came up my friendly bush baby woke me and told me she had to get back to her own hollow in the tree she called home. She had been separated from her family and they would be worried for sure. It so happens that bush babies eat similar foods to us squirrels and they also play in the trees just like we do, but only at night. Bush babies have enormous eyes so they can see better in the dark and don't really like being out in the day. That's what makes them nocturnal. I said goodbye to my new friend, and leaving me with the heartiest hug I ever could imagine, she sprung out of my hollow and was gone. I hoped one night she would come back and visit me and I also hoped that in the future no one else would land in my cosy, little nest whilst I slept.

Charlie Falls In Love

Squirrels don't keep time like humans do. We know when it's day and when it's night but we don't count to seven and then say one week, and then count those and say one month and one year. I learnt how to do that whilst staying with my family but out in the forest I forgot all about the day and night counting and soon enough I wasn't so sure how long I'd been playing and having fun in the forest of Kalumbila. I met so many new friends, and a few creatures that were definitely not going to ever be friends with me. I learnt it's safer not to be on the forest floor and got myself into the habit of staying higher up in the trees to avoid creatures who can't climb too well but would love to have squirrel on their menu if the chance presented itself. I met a rather unsavoury character on the floor of the forest once. He had small beady eyes and a forked tongue that kept shooting in and out even whilst he spoke, which he did constantly. I got that real uneasy feeling and scooted up a tree just to be safe. I'd never met such a creature, and trying not to be rude I asked him his business. He stuttered, stammered, ummmmed and ahhhhhed, so I just knew all was not as it should be. He said he was a legavaan and just wanted to help me gather a few nuts and things. He said he loved nuts too but would give them all to me if I came down and fetched them.

I scurried further up the tree and shouted back down to Mr. Legavaan that I was still searching for the Smartie tree and didn't really like those nuts anyway but thanked him all the same. I ran straight into the rear end of a squirrel on my way up and luckily didn't push her off the tree trunk altogether. She wasn't too upset about the unexpected nudge from behind and encouraged me to follow her, at a more acceptable distance, further up to the leafy canopy of the forest.

There we rested and she told me about her daughter, Lola, who had been kidnapped by the starlings. We decided to search for Lola. The Smartie tree could wait! I told Lola's mom about the human family that took in injured and abandoned forest animals and helped them get back to health so they could return to the forest again. Lola's mom was super excited to hear this and we took off immediately in the direction of the big house I grew up in. As we got closer my heart began to warm with the love I remembered from my adopted family. My mom, dad and beautiful

Keryn. Homer and Sheki the naughty twin fox terriers. Gazi and Nama, the rescued dogs. My lazy cat sisters, Smudge and Licorice, and blind Lilo whose cheerful chirping and whistling became louder and louder as we got closer and closer.

Suddenly Lola's mom stopped, and it was close, but I managed not to bump straight into her once again. There on the peanut table sat Lola. Her beauty took my breath away. She wore her strength and self-confidence like a badge.

I have felt love before but never have I ever experienced being *in love*. I could imagine how I'd fumble and stumble and fall out the tree like an idiot so I quietly stepped backwards until I had completely disappeared into the leaves, just like my friend the chameleon. Lola looked up, blinked hard as if in disbelief at what she saw and then shouted for her mom. Then the two of them raced together, laughing and crying as they embraced one another. I would have to make a plan to win Lola's heart, and just by looking at her I knew that would not be easy. I would have to clean myself up and polish up my manners but most importantly I wanted to find that Smartie tree as there was no one else in the whole world I wanted to show it to except for lovely Lola.

"I will be back." I happily shouted to no one in particular, and scampered off.

I Am Smudge Ryan

I am Smudge Ryan and I am the oldest non-human member of the Ryan family. I am even older than the youngest human member of the family, but I am the most important of them all because I am a beautiful tortoise shell cat! I have a real cat sister; her name is Licorice and she thinks she is more important than everyone but she is not. I am. I know this because I said so. I tell myself every day that I am the most important of all.

As it goes, I am the only one that listens to me. I talk and talk and talk and no one will listen. As annoying as it may be that is how it is. Here is an example of no one listening. Homer and Sheki, my naughty fox terrier brothers who are twins, never listen to me, or to anyone to be fair. When they come hurtling through the door at the same time, pushing and shoving as each one wanted to be in front of the other.

I roll my eyes up to the heavens and tell them, "one at a time boys! One at a time!" They don't listen. Instead, they both go to our water bowl and at the same time, stick their noses in and start drinking water. I've explained a million times that the water bowl is for everyone. It's a communal water bowl. Hello! Do they listen? No, they do not. They blow bubbles out their noses and splash water everywhere. They pant and snort and growl at one another and sometimes at me. I tell them to *keep it tidy chaps*. I mean who do they think is going to clean up after them?

It's certainly not my job but it is someone's job and they should be less messy, but they are not. I have even found a dog biscuit floating in the water on more than one occasion and that really annoys me. It puts the hair on my back up as I don't like getting my paws wet, which I have to do to fish it out before I can also have a sip of water. I have voiced my demand for my own water bowl but have I got my own water bowl? No, I have not! You see, no one listens to me except me. Then they all wonder why I sleep all day long. I am not really asleep, like they think I am. I am resting, but my ears are always awake and they listen very carefully to what is going on in the house or in the garden. I always know what is happening and I can tell you many stories about the Ryan family. My favourite story is a romantic one, but I know many stories about the animals that have come to stay forever and some that only stayed a short time. Most of the animals that don't stay long are from the forest and are called wild animals. They don't belong in houses where humans, dogs and cats live. They like to be wild and free out in the wilderness. The only times wild animals come to live with us is when they are abandoned or orphaned or injured and only for as long as it takes to get them to where they can leave. Some even overstay their time because they like to live here with us. I am not always happy about that.

One Hundred Years Old

Everyone who comes and stays for any amount of time calls themselves a Ryan. I am not sure who says they can, but no one asks me first. Being the most important Ryan of all it would be expected that I am consulted first, but am I? No, I am not! Take Lilo for instance. She came into the home when we stayed in a thatched roof cottage on the Zambezi River in Katima Mulilo, which is in Namibia. How do I know all this? It is because I listen very carefully when everyone thinks I am asleep. I have even been called a lazy cat which makes me smile. They don't have a clue about what I am really doing. Back to Lilo. She came along and at first, I wondered what on earth she was because someone said they had found a bird but this bird had no feathers. I know all birds have feathers. Most cats like playing with them. I am not most cats and, to be honest, I don't like feathers which means I dislike birds too. Lilo makes a lot of noise and she was quite cheeky when she first started flying. That was after her feathers grew and that's how I found out she really was a bird after all. It was too late to do anything about it by then, and she is still with us. Unfortunately for her she had an accident and is now blind, but in the beginning, she used to swoop down and try to touch me on my head whilst I was pretending to be asleep. It annoyed me a lot and once or twice I tried to smack her with my paw. My mom, who sees everything, told me not to do that because Lilo is a Ryan and lives with us too. Did I get asked if she could be a Ryan? No, I did not. She, just one day, was Lilo Ryan and she is still here, always cheerful and singing. It's enough to make my day grumpier! Lilo sits all day long in her open cage in the kitchen with her food and water bowls lined up the same way every day so she always knows exactly where everything is. Does anyone call her lazy for just being there? No, they do not! She isn't even called noisy. Quite often I hear my mom saying that her singing is beautiful. Mom really should get her ears checked. Lilo calls the dogs when they make a raucous at the gate which does happen regularly. The dustbin collectors come on a Thursday, and it is chaos for the time it takes them to empty the big, green bin by the gate. It is not only Homer and Sheki that make a din. I have two other sisters that are dogs,

You guessed it! They are Ryan's too. Gazi Ryan and Nama Ryan are two rescue dogs that came at different times to live with us. Gazi is the oldest and she thinks she knows everything but does she? No, she does not!

She does not even know that I am much older than her. She is an eleven-year-old in human years which makes her seventy-seven in dog years, because every human year is equal to seven dog years. I know my math and that seven multiplied by eleven is equal to seventy-seven. I am sixteen, and in cat years that means I am older than a hundred-year-old human.

The first two years in a cat's life are equal to twenty-five in human years and every single cat-year after that is equal to four human years. That bit of math is quite complicated, but I am quite sure it equals to more than one-hundred. It also depends on how active one is, and I would say listening is an activity, so based on that I am extremely active! Being over one-hundred, one would think I am respected. Am I respected? No, I am not!

One day this rather small, pink thing arrived and although I was interested to find out what on earth it was, I did not let anyone think I was. They might have thought my interest was somehow making this new addition important, so I waited and found my opportunity to make an enquiry much later on when the fuss around this little, pink blob had settled down. Turned out it was a squirrel baby and its mother had an unfortunate event with a cat named Gracie. I care less for squirrels. They are just as annoying as birds. When this little pip squeak grew up he used to poke me thinking I was asleep. Then he would run as fast as his little squirrel legs could run because he knew what was coming to him if I caught him. He also called himself a Ryan, Charlie Ryan.

Did anyone ask me if Charlie could be a Ryan? No, they did not. Charlie lived with us for nine months before he decided to move out to his own house in the forest. I cannot imagine what took him so long. I told him on countless occasions to go get lost in the forest, but did he listen? No, he did not listen to me because no one ever does. He still comes to visit but that's only because Lola came to stay. I can tell you their story if you have time to listen. It is a true love story and I love telling it. I don't like much but I do enjoy a good love story, especially the way I tell it.

A True Love Story

First, we had Charlie Ryan and after he went to build his own little place in a tall tree quite far from home, Lola Ryan arrived. She was not a pink little blob like Charlie when she came to the Ryan home, but I knew exactly that trouble had arrived on our doorstep. She was a feisty, head-strong girl who called herself the mighty Lola.

There was always a plan hatching in her furry, little head and she wasn't willing to share it with anyone. She didn't share anything at all, ever. One day Gertrude was cleaning up the house which she does regularly, and she cleaned up Lola's mess which she made regularly, but this time Lola got so mad she chased poor Gertrude and bit her hard. My mom came running to the rescue, but did Lola get into trouble? No, she did not.

She never got into trouble with my mom. She got cuddles and kisses for all her antics and tantrums! My mom always used to say, "we all need a little love to help us through the worst of our woes." but I wouldn't know about that as, being perfect myself, I do not have any worries.

Only dog biscuits floating in the water bowl cause me anxiety, which is totally unnecessary and so easily avoided if Homer and Sheki would just listen. I've told them both to go get lost in the forest but do they listen to me? No, they do not.

So, Lola moved in and next thing I knew she was Lola Ryan. Another addition to the Ryan family with no consent from me. Lola was always angry at someone or something. The only humans she loved and cared for were Mom and Dad. One day Lola was curled up under the covers on the sofa and I heard her talking in her sleep. Licorice said she was having a nightmare about when she was much, much younger and before she came to stay with us. The mean, old starling in the group that flies over our house did something terrible to poor Lola and she has never forgotten it. He flew off with her in his beak and then dropped her from way up there in the sky. I'm sure he didn't intend for that to happen. I can imagine Lola being the brat that she is now was also the same, if not worse, even at a young age and the starling would have thought he had pecked more than he could chew so just spat her out. Starlings are not clever like I am. I am clever because I am a cat. Important and clever should make everyone listen to me but do they listen? No, they do not.

When Lola moved in with us she was still needing her bottle which my Mom used to prepare for Keryn to feed to Lola. A baby squirrel is called a kitten and it so happens baby cats are also called kittens. Keryn is the youngest of the humans in my family and she loves all the animals that come and get to be called Ryans. She helps to take care of them all, even the big spotted eagle-owls, Bila and Kalum, who believe it or not were also allowed to be called Ryan. Did anyone ask me if they could be Ryans? No, they did not. Lola spent a lot of time with Keryn. They used to watch movies together and also share snacks and take naps on her bed. Lola had big ideas of taking over the forest but her first mission was to find her real mom. She remembered her real mom from before the starling kidnapped her and she desperately wanted to be reunited with her. I was secretly hoping she would go off to find her squirrel mom and stay with her in the forest.

I had a cat conference with Licorice to discuss how she could go beyond the gate and fence and look for Lola's mother. Licorice was quite excited to go on an adventure and she knew where there was a hole in the fence to go through. We arranged one night that she would go after her supper so no one suspected what she was up to. I waited a long time for her to return and just as I started to worry she came flying through the hole in the fence with her ear all torn. She told me that she hadn't seen a single squirrel but there were many scary creatures of the night out and about that nearly frightened her socks off, many of which she had never seen or heard during the day. That's when I remembered that there are night animals that only come out when it is dark and that they are called nocturnal animals. Squirrels only come out during the day and are called diurnal. I told Licorice she would have to go during the day, but she was so angry and her ear was sore and bleeding where she caught it on the wire when she came back home in such a mad hurry, she refused to go. So that plan was a non-starter. Lola would have to find her own missing mommy.

A Reunion of True Love

Winter in Kalumbila is dry and at night it can get quite cold. I don't really like the cold even though I have thick fur to keep me warm, so I stay indoors most of the time. Early mornings are still cool and it can get cold inside the house too. Sometimes when the sun has warmed up a bit I go out and lie on the grass where I can enjoy the warmth of the morning sun. I listen to the chitter chatter that goes on all around in the tall trees of Kalumbila and in the wild forest next to our house. I have learnt so much from the creatures that live in the forest. They are always so excited and full of energy, always on the move and telling all who will listen about what is happening in their lives. My ever-listening ears can tune in to their conversations and that is how I learn all that goes on around the garden. There are many birds just like Lilo flying around. They talk very loudly to Lilo, and Lilo talks very loudly back. She tells them what she has in her food bowls every day. It's always the same but she has to tell them that she has grapes, strawberries, banana and apple every single day! All Lilo's friends shout back that they are pleased she has grapes, strawberries, banana and apple again. Sometimes she tells them the same thing over and over and they just keep repeating what fruits she has, letting her know they are very happy to know it. As I said I find birds annoying and that is a really good reason why! They do however make a cheerful contribution to the world, so I believe they are quite necessary to have around.

There are also beautiful parrots that come to our garden. That's because my mom insists on putting fruit out on the peanut table for them. They are much bigger than Lilo and her friends and always come in twos or threes. They are not Ryans, but that is because they have not yet come in to the Ryan house to stay a while. If I said Lilo and friends were loud, then you should hear that lot. They call themselves Meyer's parrots.

They squawk, screech and whistle whenever they come around. Of all the birds, the Meyer's parrots talk the most about what goes on in the forest of Kalumbila. I get most of my information from lying about in the sun and listening to them go on about other animals' lives that, quite honestly in my opinion, is none of their business. However, it is just like listening to CNN on the TV and getting to know all the news that is currently happening. They are sometimes quite dramatic and can tell stories in conversation with one another, which is how I find out all the ins and outs of situations that take place in the forest. I found out that Charlie bumped into Lola's squirrel mom whilst he was distancing himself from the giant legavaan that hangs about here. I am afraid of that big legavaan. I hear he can whip you with his tail and has a ferocious bite. As long as he stays on his side of the forest and does not interrupt my morning sunbathe, I will be most grateful.

As the Meyer's parrots were discussing other creatures' business, I saw Charlie come through the trees with another squirrel. There are always lots of squirrels around in our garden. They hide in the creepers that grow on the trees and are so camouflaged against the browns and greys of the tree bark that sometimes it's hard to see them at all. Once you start looking and their movement catches your eye you can spot plenty of them hanging around waiting for the peanuts that get put out every day on the table underneath the big tree in our garden. Lola was also out in the garden lost in her own thoughts, sniffing the big red flowers that grow at this time of the year and playing with the water droplets that sparkled as the sun caught them. Lola loves pretty things, especially sparkly things. Even though I don't like to admit it out loud, Lola is a beautiful squirrel who loves beautiful things. She is just too bossy and also thinks she does not need to listen to me. Lola. Brave, bold, beautiful Lola, and if the Meyer's parrots had it right, she was going to be very happy indeed to meet her squirrel mom in a short while. I saw her squeeze her eyes shut and when she opened them wide, she realised it was her dear mother standing in front of her. Charlie took a step back and blended in with the leaves around him whilst Lola and her squirrel mom embraced and danced, laughed and cried together. Just as Charlie decided to leave the mother and daughter to their reunion, Lola's mom ran after him and brought him back to Lola. She excitedly told Lola how she had met Charlie and that it was all because of him that she had found her precious daughter. The crowd of squirrels surrounding them and all of Lilo's friends cheered and chirped and whooped in delight to hear of Charlie the hero's bravery and kindness.

With all this happening around them, Charlie and Lola never once stopped gazing into one another's eyes. Both of them clearly in awe of each other and equally in love. Charlie reached out and took Lola's hand in his and without a single word between them, they let each other know that this was true love at first sight. Someone in the crowd shouted Charlie's name and they all began to chant…***Charlie-Charlie-Charlie!*** The atmosphere was electric, the excitement almost tangible.

Charlie and Lola, the two squirrels who were destined to meet and fall in love. Lola fluttered her big eyelashes as if a little shy, which is something none of us had ever thought possible of her. It was as if Charlie had managed to soften the hardened edges of her heart, and her softness radiated from her. The brave and strong, beautiful Lola could also be the tender and loving, beautiful Lola. Charlie always had a charming way about him, but I had always thought of him as the baby squirrel who used to tease and taunt whomever he could find in the mornings he woke up. Charlie who loved to play and fool about had gone for a while and come back all grown up. I knew that he had his own crusade in mind, and that was to find the precious Smartie tree that he believed grew in the forest. Charlie loves smarties and all he had ever spoken about was going on an adventure to find the tree where he could taste all the smarties he could ever have dreamt of. A never-ending supply of his favourite treat. To be honest I think Charlie just found something way more precious than his Smartie tree could ever be. He felt love in his heart and his head was slowly catching up with it. Lola was way more valuable than anything Charlie could ever have thought important. Sometimes we don't always see the most prized treasure, even when it's sitting right in front of us. Charlie realised that nothing in the world was more important than his love for Lola. It looked to me that Lola felt exactly the same.

A short while after Charlie and Lola met, the whole forest knew of the love that blossomed between them. It had started as a small seed planted and nurtured, uncurled from their hearts and flourished into one heart bursting with adoration and affection, respect and love for each other. Every woodland creature eventually heard Charlie and Lola's romantic story and were enchanted by it. Charlie and Lola made their home close to the big house where they could hop, dance and race through the trees to visit us all here and help themselves to the never-ending supply of peanuts and treats left on the peanut table every day.

It wasn't too long after and Lola came home one day with her twin babies. Lola was now a mighty mom and she needed to teach her two babies how to be fierce, strong, mighty squirrels. But most importantly of all, Lola needed to teach her babies how to love with all their little squirrel hearts. Love endures all things. Love gives us hope that tomorrow is the gift we have been waiting for. The opportunity to start again and have the happiness we all deserve.

I have learnt a valuable lesson telling the love story of Charlie and Lola. There will be many more 'Ryans' to come and go in our big house and there is no doubt in my kitty head that no one will ask me first, but if they feel the unconditional love, acceptance, and forgiveness, then they deserve to be a Ryan too. That is because I have learnt that Ryan is not just a name, it's a feeling!

Charlie & Lola's

Photo Gallery

Charlie Sets Off For The Forest

Sheralee Ryan

See You Soon Mom!

Cuddles At The Peanut Table

Rise And Shine...
Or Not!!!

Lola Lovin' The Ladder

Tree Climbing Is Fun!

The Old Chameleon
Wasn't Hiding Today

Sheralee Ryan

Tender And Loving
A Beautiful Lola

Peanut Time For Me
Under The Big Tree

Sheralee Ryan

Lola Enjoying A Juicy Grape

Free In A Tree
As All Squirrels Should Be

Sheralee Ryan

Almost Done With Lunch...
Then It's Time for Dessert

Who Ate All The Peanuts?

Sheralee Ryan

Tree Fungus Makes A Great Look-out

A Little Exploration...
Is This The Smartie Tree?

Sheralee Ryan

Just One More!

Leapin' Lizards!
It's A Legavaan!
(Rock Monitor-not quite six feet)

Sheralee Ryan

Fierce, Fearless, Mighty Lola

It's A Bush Baby
Come Out To See Me

Sheralee Ryan

Waiting For More Snacks To Arrive

About the Author

Originally from Durban, South Africa, Sheralee, her husband Gary and young daughter Keryn moved to Namibia where they stayed for almost six years. Always having had a love for nature and God's beautiful creatures, Namibia provided the opportunity for the Ryan family to experience wildlife first hand. For the first two years, they lived in a cottage on a fish farm on the Zambezi River. In 2015 the family moved on to Gobabis, 200 kilometres east of Windhoek where they were involved with the Gobabis Animal Rescue, helping and caring for animals in need. At the end of 2018, they moved to Kalumbila, North West Province of Zambia where their interaction with nature continues and, where possible, they have assisted injured animals to rehabilitate and release them back into the wild. Charlie's amazing personality inspired Sheralee to write his story, from his point of view naturally.

Other Works

For The Latest Information On

What is Available

New Releases

&

Coming Soon

Please Visit

JasamiPublishingLtd.com

In the Next Adventure...

Lola's Twins
Eating a Grape

Sheralee Ryan

Printed in Great Britain
by Amazon